Like Mr Peabody in this story, **Val Biro** is a painter and he likes animals. He is also an author and illustrator who is perhaps best known for his 'Gumdrop' stories, which are all based on his own vintage car.

Val was born in Hungary but now lives in Sussex with his wife Mimi, who took the photograph on the back cover.

British Library Cataloguing in Publication Data
Biro, Val
    Drango dragon
    Rn: Balint, Stephen Biro
    I. Title
    823'.914[J]
    ISBN 0-7214-9596-6

First edition
Published by Ladybird Books Ltd Loughborough Leicestershire UK
Ladybird Books Inc Auburn Maine 04210 USA
Printed in England

DRANGO DRAGON

story and pictures
by VAL BIRO

Ladybird Books

Mr Peabody was an artist.
He painted pictures of dogs
and elephants and crocodiles,
because he liked animals.
But he enjoyed painting
dragons even more, because
he liked dragons best of all.

The trouble was that he had
no animals to paint *from*,
not even a dog.
And certainly no dragons.

So his pictures weren't very good
and nobody wanted
to buy them.

One day there was a knock at his door. An old gypsy woman stood there with her horse and van. 'Buy a trinket from old Nell,' she said, 'and you will find that all goes well.'

Mr Peabody
had no need of
bracelets or bangle
nor even clothes pe
or tin kettl

But he not
a dog in the
A dog! Now that
just what he war
It looked frier
the gypsy woman was willing to s
so he bought it there and t

The dog's name was Gordan. 'I got him off a miner,' the old woman had said in her funny way, 'but I think he comes from China.' Chinese or not, Gordan was a very nice little dog.

Mr Peabody was delighted. 'Now I have a *real* dog to paint from!' And he gave Gordan a bowl of biscuits and a bone.

The dog finished his biscuits in no time and settled down happily with his bone.

Mr Peabody began to paint – and it was the finest
dog picture he had ever done.

Next day he showed it to Mr Brisket-Barker, the dog breeder. 'What a fine Chinese dog,' he said and promptly bought the picture.

Mr Peabody was so pleased that he went straight back to paint some more pictures of Gordan. He showed them to Mr Brisket-Barker, and the dog breeder bought every one.

'You've brought me luck!' said Mr Peabody to Gordan that night. 'You are my best friend now, but there's just one thing — I don't like your name.' And he sat down to think of a new one. 'I know! I could make anagrams of your name!' He called them out and it sounded like a chant:

Gordan
Gadron
Randog
Ragdon
Dogran
Dagron
Drango
Dragon...

'That's it!' he shouted. 'DRANGO DRAGON!'

And then a remarkable thing happened. Right in front of his eyes the dog began to change.

His body grew long,
his coat went scaly,
his feet became claws,
his colour turned green
and his tail curled
right up behind him.

And there he stood at last,
red wings and all, a large
and genuine Chinese Dragon!

'Thank you very much,'
said the dragon with a
toothy grin. 'You've
broken the ancient Chinese
spell that had turned me
into a little dog. I feel a
lot better now!'

Mr Peabody was astounded.
A dragon! 'Now I have a
real dragon to paint from!'
He danced with joy and
got out his brushes.

But Drango Dragon was hungry and he didn't fancy dog biscuits now.

So he walked to the fireplace and helped himself to a large lump of coal. 'My favourite dish,' he said, smacking his lips. So Mr Peabody fetched a whole bucketful and as Drango munched, Mr Peabody painted.

Having finished his meal, Drango Dragon sat down, ate a box of matches for afters and leaned back, puffing at a pipe with his own smoke. He looked very content and Mr Peabody painted another picture.

Then the dragon wanted to try out
his wings so he flew round and round
the garden and back again. All the
time Mr Peabody painted, and they were
the finest dragon pictures he had ever done.

Next day Mr Peabody took the pictures to the Art Gallery and showed them to Mr Dealer-Varnish, who promptly bought them all.

'If you can paint some more like these,' he said, 'people will queue up to buy them!'

Mr Peabody was delighted. He bought a sackful of matches for
Drango and ordered a lorryload of coal.
Then he painted more pictures of
Drango and they were better
than ever.

After dinner they sat down
by the fire (which the dragon
had lit with his hot breath)
and Drango told him
stories of old China.

When Mr Peabody had enough new pictures he took them to the Art Gallery, and Drango Dragon came with him. Sure enough, soon there was a queue. People recognised Drango from the pictures and asked for his autograph.

But others who had not heard of him were terrified to see a large dragon puffing smoke, and ran for their lives. They didn't know what a friendly dragon Drango really was.

Early one morning there was real trouble. Drango decided to go out for a walk all by himself.

He went past a field, but the smell of hay made his nose tickle – and he sneezed!
His hot breath set a barn on fire and the farmer, who came running out, was absolutely furious.

Drango flew home as fast as
he could and told Mr Peabody,
who rang the fire brigade.

Drango was alarmed when he saw the angry
farmer coming up the road after him. And that
meant trouble for Mr Peabody too! 'There's only
one thing to do now,' said Drango. 'Please say all
my names again, but backwards. Quick!'

So Mr Peabody began to chant:

> Dragon
> Drango
> Dagron
> Dogran
> Ragdon
> Randog
> Gadron
> Gordan...

And to his amazement Drango Dragon disappeared! Instead of the dragon, there stood little Gordan the dog.

He was exactly the same as before, except that he could speak now.

Just then the farmer burst in. 'Where's that dreadful dragon of yours?' he bellowed.

'There is no dragon here,' said Mr Peabody truthfully. 'But as I am a rich dragon-painter now, allow me to pay for your barn.' And the farmer walked away with the money, feeling much better. Whew! What a relief!

Now that the danger was over, Gordan the dog was itching to become a dragon once more. So Mr Peabody chanted out the names again – in the right order this time – and there stood Drango, red wings and all! It was really quite amazing!

But he looked thoughtful. 'This might get into the papers and there will be a lot of fuss and bother. It would save you trouble if I went on a short holiday. Anyway, I want to visit my old friends in China.'

Mr Peabody agreed. He was so good at dragon pictures by now that he could paint them without a real dragon for a while.

So he gave Drango a bucket of coal for the journey, and plenty of matches. 'But don't worry!' said the dragon with a toothy grin. 'I'll be back soon!' And they shook hands like old friends.

And so it was that Drango Dragon walked out of the house, stretched his red wings and flew away towards the rising sun.